MW00908498

Romance: Her Billionaire Boss

Kelli Sloan

Romance: Her Billionaire Boss

Kelli Sloan

Copyright © 2015

Published by Run Free Publishing

All rights reserved.

No part of this publication may be reproduced, stored in a retrieval system, or transmitted, in any form or by any means without the prior permission in writing of the publisher.

This is a work of fiction. Any resemblance to any person, living or dead, is purely coincidental.

For Max – May the world never forget you.

Also by Kelli Sloan:

Romance: Housekeeper for the Billionaire

Romance: The Billionaire's Lust

Romance: The Billionaire's Secrets

Romance: The Billionaire's Desire

Romance: Working for the Billionaire's Pleasure

Romance: Her Billionaire Boss

Kelli Sloan

Chapter 1

Damn.

I've lost another file.

He isn't going to be happy. Actually, *he* is probably going to be quite mad.

Brock Maxton is known for his furious anger. It was only yesterday that I saw him throw an office chair in a boardroom meeting, barely missing a million dollar piece of artwork. Not that I thought the tiny piece of artwork was worth a million dollars. I actually thought his niece or nephew did the painting. Why anyone would pay a million dollars for a few wild brushstrokes on small black canvas is beyond me. Obviously I chose the wrong profession.

I've only had this job for a week and I've already experienced so much. I love this job… well, I love what happened to my bank account when the first paycheck was received. The pay is more than four times what I made at my old job.

There is just one problem… I'm horrible at this job.

I thought being a personal assistant to a billionaire investor would be easy work. I thought that life would be all cocktail parties, organizing rounds of golf and taking notes while flying in personal jets.

Turns out, I was wrong.

I couldn't have been further from the truth.

Brock works all of his personal assistants hard. There are four of us and he makes full use of our time. There is no time to sit around and gossip about the latest book I've read. Nope, this isn't a casual book club. Then again, I'm not sure if the other three assistants have ever read a book. They don't seem like the reading type.

But they are better at this job than I am.

They deliver what Brock wants on time, every time. Sometimes, they have what he wants ready before he even asks for it. They smile their flawless smiles, dress their slim bodies perfectly and giggle like schoolgirls when he walks past.

Whereas I deliver coffee late, spill water on important photocopies, and I always seem to be losing files like the one that I can't find right now.

I'm quite surprised that he hasn't fired me yet.

I'm trying so hard because I need the money, but it seems the harder I try, the more I fail. It's the highest paying job I've had to date and with the price of rent, I have to try everything in my power to keep the position.

I continue to look for the elusive file and a couple of other of the assistants are laughing and talking behind my back. Despite their snickering laughter, I am determined to keep going and will do anything to prevent failure.

The door to Brock's office swings opens and their bitchy laughter instantly stops.

Brock has a presence about him. Whenever he walks into a room, people pay attention. He is tall, broad and his physique is dominant.

"Bella. I need you to stay late tonight and type up these files."

Brock's large hands fling three files to my desk and they land with a heavy thud.

"I'll get right on it, sir," I say, trying to keep my composure while hoping and praying that he doesn't ask for the file that I have just lost.

He nods his head slightly and walks back into his office.

"She's definitely going to screw that up," whispers one of the assistants.

"I'm pretty sure that she would lose her head if it wasn't attached to her body," another one laughs.

"She's definitely going to be a goner. Girls like her aren't cut out for intense jobs like this. She probably slept with someone to get the job," says another one just loud enough for me to hear.

I shoot them a glare but they stare back. They are very well drilled at cutting stares. They could probably do that for a living.

I hold my tongue and don't say anything because I don't want to make a scene. I don't care what they say - I will get better at this job. I know I will.

I'm a hard worker and I can do this.

I open up the files that Brock dumped on my desk and begin typing as fast as I can - which really isn't that fast at all - but my fingers are trying.

As my digits pound the keyboard, I hear all the girls gathering up their things to go out for after-work drinks. It's bad enough that I didn't receive an invite, but they don't have to rub my face in it. They could at least keep it quiet around me.

I don't even like the girls that I'm working with, but that doesn't mean I don't want to be invited. If this is where I am going to have spend sixty hours a week, I would like to at least pretend we could be friends.

It would be nice to be accepted by this group of supermodel personal assistants.

As the elevator door closes behind them, my eyes fill with tears.

Damn.

Why does it upset me?

I don't even like them. I don't want to go to drinks with them.

Actually, I think dipping my fingers into acid would be more fun than hanging out with them. They will probably sit at the bar, sip expensive cocktails and talk about which girls are dressed badly at the bar, all the while waiting for the next guy that is going to sweep them off their feet.

I don't want that. I don't want to be part of that lifestyle.

That's not me.

But it doesn't stop my eyes from filling with tears of rejection.

If those girls are princesses, then I'm a boxer.

I fight until nothing is left to give. That's why I think I'll be good at this job. I just have to try and get used to the pace of the work first.

And I will.

I'm determined to.

The last two weeks have been so fast and intense. There has been so much pressure on me that I think I could fall apart at any second.

Wiping my eyes in the empty office, I hear Brock's door violently swing open again.

"Where are the files? I need them now!" Brock yells.

He glares at me with a fire in his eyes that sends chills down my spine.

I peel my eyes off him and look back at the screen where I've just started typing the second page of the first file. I was hoping I'd have a little bit more time but it's clear that I was wrong. My time's up and it may cost me my job.

"Um... they aren't done yet, sir, but I will have them done soon."

I hope that it will buy me some time but you never know with a man like him. He likes things done right then and there which is another reason why I suck at this job. I am like a tortoise and he is like a hare.

He sighs heavily in frustration.

"You are hopeless. Just plain hopeless," his head shakes. "You are about to lose your job - I hope that you know that. I don't know how much more incompetence I can put up with. You have driven me completely insane!"

I look at him in disbelief but I know what he says is true.

Doesn't mean it stings any less though.

I was hoping I could just slide by, and while all the other robot assistants were doing good work, my bad work wouldn't be as noticeable...

But it is completely the opposite.

"Hopeless! Who the hell hired you?!"

The fire in his eyes makes my insides burn.

I know that I should just apologize, put my head down and work harder.

That's what the princess personal assistants would do.

But that's not me.

No way.

That's not how I work.

"You put unreasonable demands on your staff!" I bite back at him, "How do you expect us to get everything done in such a short amount of time? We aren't robots! Well at least not all of us are. Some of us need time to make sure that it's right - not speed through the work just to be on your good side!"

He raises his brow in surprise and I can sense the frustration ooze off him.

Nobody ever raises their voice to him, let alone talks to him the way that I just did.

"Every single one of my assistants, except for you, gets what needs to be done finished. Sometimes, they finish even before it has to be finished. You're the only one who seems to be having a problem here. I'm questioning why you were hired in the first place because you haven't been assisting or helping me with anything at all. Honestly, you've been holding me back. My other assistants have to finish what you mess up," his jaw grins in anger.

"I was hired because I work hard and never give up on a task. I am the hardest working woman you will ever meet. No one works harder than me," I say defiantly, standing up from behind my desk.

I know that arguing with him is a bad idea but he had to respect me for stating what everybody else was scared to say.

He stares at me and shakes his head. The frustration is going away but some aggravation is still lingering there.

"You could indeed be the hardest worker alive… or my hiring chief just thought that you would be nice to look at. Wouldn't be the first time it's happened and I know that it won't be the last. I don't deny that you work hard but you just aren't a very productive assistant. That's not good for my team. I need the members of my team to be movers and shakers."

I sigh.

I am losing the argument but there is no way that I can walk away.

Not yet.

I desperately need this job and I'm going to keep it if it's the last thing I do.

"Look, I know I'm not the perfect assistant. I don't get things done on time. I'm always losing something or dropping things but I am not leaving this job. I love it here and I've given it everything I have. I will get better, I know it, and I will do anything to keep this job. Anything!" I plead with him.

"Anything?" he asks with a raised brow.

Oh no.

That was the wrong choice of words…

⁇

Chapter 2

I have a feeling I'm going to regret using the word 'anything'. I can tell by the look in his eyes.

It looks like trouble.

What if he wants me to do something illegal?

What if he secretly works for the mob and needs someone to be a hired killer?

Oh, who cares? I will work for the money. I will do what I have to do to keep this job.

I will.

No matter what he wants, I am going to do it.

And he is a billionaire - surely he wouldn't risk everything he has over something illegal, right? Then again, that's what rich people are known for.

Damn!

"Yes, I'll do almost anything to keep working for you," I say, looking him straight in his eyes hoping that this won't be a decision that I'll regret.

"Almost anything? Or anything?" he asks while studying me.

"Um… anything," I reply.

He nods his head and a slight smirk comes across his beautiful face.

"Clearly, you are not cut out for the office and since this is all about business, I can't have you working here. You are a liability here. I need this office to run very smoothly. This is an investment firm and I need to know that everyone can hold their own… and you can't."

"But?" I ask in hope of another offer.

"There is, however, a chance for you to work for me privately. There is less stress and no office work. That should be the perfect job for you because it doesn't actually take any real skill."

"Privately?" I ask, ignoring the attack on my office abilities.

I hadn't heard of anyone working for him privately. Maybe there was a reason why?

"You can be the personal assistant at my penthouse. It's less stress and you won't have to become unemployed. It's a win–win situation."

"What will I do around your penthouse?" I ask curiously.

I've never heard of a penthouse assistant and wanted to be sure that it wasn't anything crazy but then again, he did say it didn't require any real skill so maybe it is just what I need.

"You need to make sure that everything runs smoothly. I'll go into more detail once you start the job tomorrow," he states as his grin widens.

"Okay… well…. I'll take it. Is the pay the same?" I ask.

It really doesn't matter if it is, any job for him would pay more than the job I used to have down at the fast food restaurant.

"It pays a little bit more…"

I nod. "Great, well, thanks. I'll… um… see you tomorrow at your penthouse then?"

"Be there at seven o'clock in the morning. I will text you the address tonight," he states.

"Okay. I will be there on time. I promise I won't let you down," I say.

"I hope not because this is your last chance," he says with a raised brow.

"Trust me, I won't let you down," I say.

He nods his head and goes back into his office. As soon as he is out of sight, I gather up my things and head towards the elevator.

I can't believe that I will be working in his house!

That is a dream come true.

I will be away from his robot assistants, crazy office work, crazy hours and I'll be doing something that I might actually be good at.

Well, hopefully, because I really didn't want to lose another job.

This is his way of giving me a second chance. I must not disappoint him.

I get onto the elevator and mash the button for the lobby, smiling all the way down. Tomorrow is going to be a good day for sure.

Hopefully.

On my way home I can't help but think about the twinkle in Brock's eyes when he offered me the job, but there was something else behind that look as well.

Something dark and dangerous.

At least that is what it seemed like.

Or maybe I was just staring at him too hard and seeing something that wasn't actually there.

I had the tendencies to do that whenever he was around and it got worse every day. I couldn't help it because the guy was like an Adonis of some sort and was probably supposed to be on display somewhere for people to admire. I know I would pay to see a statue of him standing in an art gallery.

I pull into my spot at my apartment complex and see that my roommate Naomi is home. I'm glad because I need to talk to her about my day. I walk in and find my roommate Naomi dancing and singing around the room listening to music loudly.

"Hi," I state over the music.

"Oh! Hi!" she shouts back as she goes to turn the tunes down.

"Good day?" I ask her.

"Nope," she replies. "I was dancing to forget."

"Doesn't sound good."

"Same old problems with my boss. Why are you getting home so late? You usually beat me home. Rough day at the office? Is your boss becoming a slave driver like mine? Although your boss is fine and I'm sure I wouldn't mind working all kinds of hours if it meant I got to look at him while I was doing it!" she giggles.

"I had to work late. I had to type up some files and since you know my typing skills are sub-par you can understand why it took me so long."

She laughs. "Oh, I can only imagine how it went. You type like two words a minute? You know you and office work don't exactly get along. I'm surprised that you have even lasted a week. Last time you had an office job you couldn't even get the photocopier to work so it shocked me when you decided to try it again."

"I know but the office job is finished now."

"Why? Were you fired?"

"No," I can't contain the smile. "I have another job now."

"Do tell..."

"Brock wants me to be the personal assistant at his penthouse."

"Oh really... and why is that?" she asks curiously.

I sigh. "Because I suck at office work and he wants me far away from the office as possible."

She laughs again. "I knew it! I knew he would eventually get tired of you at the office. So what will you be doing at his house?"

"He says making sure everything runs smoothly and that he will tell me more when I go over there tomorrow. He says that it doesn't take any real skill so I'm sure that it's the perfect job for me."

She nods her head. "I knew it was only going to be a matter of time before your clumsiness got the best of you. How did you even manage to get that office job in the first place? It's a competitive position. Brock is a billionaire so I figured he would only hire people with experience. No offense but well… you are… you. You must've given one killer interview."

I walk into the kitchen and grab a bottle of water.

"He didn't exactly hire me. His hiring director did and I begged and pleaded for that job. Told him I was a hard worker and he would never find anyone who worked harder than me. He believed me but Brock seems to think that I was hired because of my looks and that his hiring director just wanted something pretty to look at."

She laughs and I roll my eyes.

"It's true, you are a hard worker, but still. You should've known it was going to be a disaster. As for you getting the job because of your looks, it wouldn't be the first time that a woman has gotten a job because she was beautiful and it won't be the last time it happens either."

"I take what I can get," I smile.

"And how's the pay for this new job? Is it the same as the office job or is it less? Either way, I'm pretty sure any job for him pays a pretty penny."

"He says that it pays a little bit more. So it sounds easy enough to me," I say as I finish off my bottled water and throw it in the trashcan.

"Which is code for I'll pay you anything to keep you from making things in my office fall apart," Naomi comments with a laugh. "He may have created a position for you and needs tonight to think of an actual job description and to figure out what exactly he will have you do."

I open the cookie jar and pick out one of the chocolate chip cookies we'd made the night before. "Either way I know all of the other assistants will be happy. They never liked me anyway and I didn't care for them either. They thought they were all that ad more."

"None of them liked you? That's their loss. You are a beautiful person," Naomi says.

I can always count on her to boost my confidence.

"They all hated me. I didn't have one single friend in the whole office. And they didn't care about getting to know me either. All they cared about was looking good in front of Brock," I say.

"Well maybe you can find someone nicer at the penthouse."

"I think I will do better work there too. There won't be as much pressure with files, deadlines, photocopying, and everything else that goes on in the office."

"If anything, you will get to see the inside of a billionaire's penthouse. I can only imagine what it looks like."

"I've never seen anything other than these small little apartments we've been living in since college."

"Hey! Our apartment isn't all that small."

"I bet our apartment could fit in the bathroom of his penthouse and then he'd still have a lot of room left over," I laugh. "I guess I'll find out tomorrow how big it is."

"I bet it's very big…" Naomi has a deviant look in her eyes.

"Not that!" I laugh again.

She shrugs her shoulders. "But I'm sure that's big too. That's what the gossip magazines say."

I roll my eyes and look at the clock. It's eleven o'clock already.

"I'm going to take a quick shower and go to bed, so that I'm ready for tomorrow. Talk to you later, gorgeous."

Pulling out a pair of pajamas, I head to the bathroom to take a quick shower then pick out an outfit to wear to work tomorrow.

I don't know how I should dress but I know that it would have to be less casual than what I wear at the office. I pull out a pair of black jeans and a white shirt with a black blazer. It is casual enough to be an assistant but still kind of professional. I set my alarm and lay back in my bed to hopefully get some rest.

My legs lay restless for what seems like forever but eventually I doze off to sleep.

☐

Chapter 3

The next morning I wake before the sun starts to stream through my windows to ensure that I make it to the penthouse on time.

Brock texted the address to my phone last night and luckily it was just a short distance from my apartment. He also texted me the information on how to get up into his penthouse suite because you need a code to enter. I hope it isn't to complex to punch in – I have never been in a house that requires a code before.

I take a quick shower, run the brush through my wild morning hair, brush my teeth, put on the clothes that I had laid out last night and grab a yogurt out of the refrigerator for breakfast. Naomi walks in the kitchen with a smile on her face and I smile back at her.

"So are you ready for your first day as penthouse assistant?" she asks as she grabs a banana off the counter.

"I hope so! I'm really nervous though. What if I mess up?" I ask as I begin to eat the yogurt.

I can barely taste it because my nerves are on overdrive but I know that I have to eat something to be on top of my game. Nobody can be productive on an empty stomach.

"Don't worry about it. What's the worst that can happen?" she says with a smirk.

"I get fired after one day," I reply.

She shrugs her shoulders, "All you can do is try."

"I really want to keep this job. If I don't, we won't be able to make rent and this is one of the nicer apartments that we've had. I fully intend on staying here for as long as possible," I say tossing the yogurt cup into the trash and placing the spoon in the sink.

"That's right so you better make sure you work your little fingers to the bone and do whatever he wants because we can't be homeless on the streets and begging people for change. That wouldn't look good for either of us. Plus, I've grown accustomed to hot showers, hot meals, TV and all the other necessities that life has to offer," she says.

I roll my eyes.

This girl has a thing for the dramatics but that's what I love about her. It is always entertaining to watch her go off on a different tangent.

"I wouldn't say that we will be on the streets begging for change but we definitely would have to downsize."

"Downsize to what? One of those studio apartments? They are just as high as a two bedroom you know and they are like a box - everything is in the same spot. We'll have to buy a pullout couch to share and you know you snore. Nope. You have to hold onto this new job so we can keep our separate bedrooms – for both of our sakes," she says as she finishes up her banana.

I shake my head.

While she was right about the studio apartment, I knew that we probably could get a cheaper two bedroom apartment but I will let her have her moment since she rarely gets to be dramatic anymore with all of the crazy hours her boss makes her work.

"Well, let me leave so that I can get to work on time so we won't be living on the streets. That should put your mind at ease."

"Good girl because neither one of us is built for dumpster diving. I don't want to have to fight a homeless guy over a half-eaten piece of chicken and some cold pizza. I do want to have some kind of dignity left, you know. And the homeless guy would probably win too because he was out there longer and then we'd be all hungry and cold and stink."

I burst out laughing as I walk out of the door.

I wave my hand and close the door behind me before she continues talking about her nightmare of being homeless. If I listen to her much longer I know I'll be rolling around on the floor laughing, which will cause me to be late for work. That's not the impression I want to give, especially since Brock is giving me a second chance.

Butterflies fill my stomach and my hands twitch endlessly with nerves as I drive to Brock's penthouse. After pulling into the parking garage, I get out and apprehensively press the code in the elevator for his suite.

The elevator fills so cold, empty, sterile and lifeless. What am I getting myself in for?

The closer the ride gets to his penthouse, the more anxious I become. My heart rate is rapidly increasing, my body temperature is rising and the shakes are starting to develop. Maybe I should just turn around now?

At least that will save the embarrassment of another failed job.

But once the elevator doors open, my nerves float away.

The doors slowly open to blinding light and I feel like I'm stepping out into heaven.

Wow.

Once my eyes adjust to the brightness, I realize how amazing this penthouse is. My mouth drops open in awe at the wide-open and spacious apartment.

"People actually live like this?" I whisper to myself.

There's glass furniture everywhere, which scares me because of my clumsiness. There are black leather chairs spread out in the opening and a winding staircase directly behind them. Even from the elevator I can see that he has an amazing view of the city skyline. Tall glass windows dominate the other side of the room. He also has a few indoor plants around his house, which really set the tone for the manly vibe that he's going for.

I step out of the elevator to get a better view.

My mouth drops even further.

This is breathtaking.

If this is how the rich live then I need to figure out a way to bump my pay grade up fast because this place is pure luxury. I want all of this.

"I didn't think people actually lived like this," I whisper in awe.

I hear someone clear their throat behind me and I spin around to see Brock standing there with his arms folded.

Again I am breathless.

Instead of his usual business suit, today Brock has on a pair of black slacks and a white t-shirt that shapes his muscular physique perfectly. It makes him seem almost approachable and not the hard working machine that I usually see at the office.

This version seems... human.

"Um... good morning, Mr. Maxton," I say. I feel like I should curtsy in his presence. "I'm ready to start and I promise you that you won't regret letting me do this."

He raises his brow and looks at me kind of funny but then it quickly disappears as if it was never there in the first place.

I stand at the doorway, waiting for further instructions. I dare not walk where I am not allowed.

A few moments later he returns.

"What you will do here is make sure that cleaners come and go on time, order food when I ask for breakfast, lunch, and dinner because I'm in between chefs right now, tidy up a little bit and make sure that everything remains exactly how it's supposed to remain. Also, be sure that no one steals anything. I've had a few things go missing in the past couple of weeks and I want to make sure that nothing else disappears," he says.

"Okay. I'll get right on it. Do you have a list of things that need to be done today?" I ask.

"There's a schedule next to the fridge for when everyone is supposed to arrive and when they are supposed to leave. There is also a few numbers on there from my favorite restaurants and what to order for them and how to pay for it. Look it over and make sure that it all happens smoothly. I'll be in my office and please try not to break anything. All of this stuff expensive. I will deduct any replacements from your paycheck."

I nod my head. "Yes sir. I won't break anything because I'm sure that it will take a lot of my paychecks to cover it."

"Okay, you can start by ordering breakfast on the schedule and bring it to me in my office," he says as he turns around and heads towards his penthouse office.

I grab the schedule next to the refrigerator and look it over. It seems easy enough to handle. Not much to do other than make sure that everything runs smoothly.

I pick up my cell phone and place the breakfast order for Brock. He wants eggs benedict with extra hollandaise sauce, turkey bacon, warm apple slices, and a honey biscuit.

I had to admit his breakfast order was a lot better than anything I've ever eaten but I'm pretty sure that it meant nothing to him. I hang up the phone and continue to look around the penthouse.

The breakfast wouldn't arrive for thirty minutes and the maid wasn't due to start for another hour.

As I look around, I see the walls that hold a lot of impressive paintings, but he has no pictures of himself or his family. I see pictures with business partners and clients but no photos of his parents or anything that would hint that he even has a life outside of his business.

I knew that his parents were still alive because of a recent magazine article I read but I guess they aren't that close.

In my apartment, on the other hand, you can find pictures of me with my parents and friends on vacation and various other places. Same with Naomi. We were both close to our parents and we made sure that our apartment felt like a home.

This place seemed like a sterile museum. Set-up to look good but not to do much of anything else in it.

"All work and no play," I mumble to myself as I look at another picture of him shaking hands with the mayor.

An intercom goes off and I go to answer it. It must be Brock's food because everyone else uses the service elevator. Only people who didn't normally work for him rang the intercom.

"Mr. Maxton's residence, may I help you?" I ask in my best professional voice.

"Yes, I have his breakfast order," says a male voice from the other side.

"Okay hold on please." I rush to grab the schedule off of the counter where I left it and press the code so that the guy can come up. "Come on up."

There is a gentle knock on the door and I open it quickly. The guy hands me the bag and a receipt to sign. I check the order to make sure that it's correct and then I walk to the direction that he went for his office.

As I approach his expansive office, I see him sitting behind a large mahogany desk. I tap lightly on the door and place his breakfast on the desk in front of him. He looks up at me and I think I see a smile on his face but it disappears so quickly that I almost think I imagined it.

"I need a glass of orange juice," he states firmly as he starts to take out his breakfast and situate it on his desk.

"Yes, sir," I say as I turn and head out of the room, back to the kitchen.

I will have to make sure that I remember the way around here because I could easily get lost in this place. Maybe I should leave a trail of breadcrumbs like Hansel and Gretel?

After filling the glass three quarters full, I spill a drop on the bench. Ignoring it, I slowly walk the glass to him and place it on the desk.

It is a miracle that I didn't spill a drop during the walk back to his office. Usually, I would have spilt half the glass on a walk that long.

"Anything else?" I ask as I stand to attention, waiting for him to answer.

"No. That will be all for now," he says as he dismisses me from the room.

"Okay... well let me know if you need anything else," I say as I walk out of the door.

Smiling to myself, I'm glad that I didn't break anything in the kitchen and that my full paycheck is still intact.

One task down. Alright.

Time for my confidence to start rising.

I go to look at the schedule to get started on my other tasks now that I've accomplished the first one. Surprisingly, the rest of the day goes by smoothly with no mishaps other than spilling the drop of orange juice.

Wow.

I'm so proud of myself.

The maid came in later in the day and she was actually very nice. So were the other people who came and went through the day. It felt so different not having to compete with my workmates for attention.

I think that I may survive this job after all and maybe even make a few friends in the process. I know that in my other job, I wasn't well liked but now I see that they weren't really my type of people anyway.

With a smile stretched across my face, I grab my purse and pack up to head home after a successful day. Brock comes out from his office and grabs a bottled water out of the refrigerator. He takes a long sip from it as he stares at me.

"Nice job, Bella. I was pleasantly surprised at your work today. See you tomorrow. We may have found a job for you yet," he says as he heads to the back towards his office.

The statement makes me jump with joy inside.

Wow.

I can do something.

I can actually do something.

Chapter 4

On my drive home, I keep thinking about the other office assistants.

If they could see me now, they would be so jealous. At one point during the day, I thought about taking a selfie outside of his office and emailing it to the office staff.

But, in the interest of keeping my current job, I decided against it.

When I pull in to my apartment, I see Naomi slowly climbing out of her car. I look at her and she looks like she had a rough day. Her hair is pulled out of its usual ponytail and I can see frustration in her eyes.

She works at a magazine and is always on crazy deadlines or chasing the next story.

"Late day at work?" I ask her as I meet her up the driveway.

"You know my boss is a slave driver and it seems to be getting worse and worse every day. I really hate her and you know that it takes a lot for me to hate someone. But that woman… ugh… she can definitely work a nerve. Especially mine."

She opens the door, walks to the fridge and grabs a wine cooler, tossing one to me. She opens hers and drinks it halfway before placing it down on the counter. "So how was your first day as penthouse assistant? Hopefully it was better than my day from hell."

I take a sip of my wine cooler. "It was good. I didn't break anything and I was on time. It actually went smoothly and I think the maid is pretty cool. There is no stress and no pressure. I think this is the job that they should've given me first and then they would've never had any problems out of me."

She laughs. "So you may have finally found a job that fits you? That's a miracle in itself."

"I think so. I really like it. I think that this is something I can do long term. He was right when he said it doesn't really require skill. I order his meals and make sure that the maid and all the other people who work for him do what they need to do. It's a piece of cake."

"That's good to know. I'm glad that the little bird has finally blossomed and gotten a job where she can handle herself. Sooo... how did the penthouse look? I've been dying for you to tell me all day. It's probably why I found my boss so annoying today. Not like I don't find her annoying on any other day though."

A smile spreads across my face as I think about how beautiful the penthouse was.

"It was huge and gorgeous, like something out of a high-end magazine. He has a lot of glass furniture and expensive paintings. He even has a few indoor trees in his apartment. And his appliances blend into the décor I almost didn't notice them at first. When I say that it was nice, I mean that it was nice!"

"I bet so. I can imagine it right now. Gosh you are so lucky! I would do anything to work for your handsome boss instead of my pain in the neck boss."

"I know."

"So don't screw it up now that you're my lifeline to the rich and famous," she says with a laugh.

I laugh. "I won't. I said I'll do anything to keep this job and I mean it. So was your day really that bad? When I pulled in the driveway you seem extremely frustrated."

"I'm telling you my boss is just evil. I worked my ass off to get to where I'm at and now all of a sudden she's trying to give me puff pieces. You know that I haven't done those since when I first started out."

"What made her want to give you the puff pieces when you usually cover what's hot in entertainment?"

She finishes off her wine cooler and grabs another one. "I think that she's jealous of me. I've been getting a lot of attention from the big heads and now I think that she resents me."

"Have you thought about going freelance?"

"I have but it's a lot of work. Besides I like belonging to a team. I like everyone except her. I just wish that she'd let up on me."

"I'm sure that it'll get better. Maybe she's going through a phase."

"Well then she's been going through a phase for about three months and needs to find a way to get over it before I say something that causes me to lose my job. And it's not just me she's rude to, it's all of the people that have been there for a while. It's as if she wants us all to disappear but she knows that if we quit, the magazine will go downhill fast."

"Stick it out until you find something better then. I know there are other magazines out there that would be happy to have you. You are wonderful, smart, funny and witty. You deserve the best job you can get."

She nods her head. "I guess you're right. Thanks for the advice. I'm about to call it a night though because with the day I've had, I need to sleep so that I don't go loco on this lady at the office tomorrow."

I laugh. "Alright. Good night."

"Good night," she says as she heads back to her room with her wine cooler in hand.

I am lucky. Very lucky.

And I plan not to stuff it up this time. I've definitely found a job where I fit in and I like it.

I really like it.

Things are looking up for me and I'm sure things will only get better from here on out.

But then, things never seem to go well in my life for long...

⍰

Chapter 5

Friday approaches quickly and everything in the penthouse is still going smoothly.

I'm thankful that I made it a full week without messing up and I still have a full paycheck to look forward to. As his personal assistant in the office, I didn't even make it a day without breaking a coffee mug or spilling something on the files.

Luckily there isn't so much pressure here and I am able to relax a little.

Plus the snickers gone from behind my back give me a tremendous confidence boost. Nobody here is waiting for me to fail and I like that.

As the week comes to a close, I pack up my things and prepare to leave when Brock comes up the elevator. He has been out most of the day so I'm surprised to see him.

"Good night, Mr. Maxton," I say as I walk towards the service elevator.

"Bella. I need you to work later tonight," he states as he stares at me directly in my eyes.

"Um… sure," I say trying to think if I forgot something from the schedule but I know that I didn't.

I pretty much had the same routine all week and I was positive that I knocked it all out.

He smirks. "You're not in trouble. I want to get to know you a little better, that's all."

"Okay," I say as I place my purse down on the table beside me.

He walks into the kitchen and pulls out a bottle of wine from the top of the cabinet, and grabs two wine glasses. He pours a glass and hands to me, without even asking if I would like it.

I take a small sip and my mouth becomes alive with flavor. Every single taste bud is blooming with the delicate sensations from the wine.

"What is this?" I ask.

I have never known wine to taste so luxurious and full.

Brock studies the bottle with raised eyebrows, "It's expensive."

I nod and I hope he doesn't see that my hands are shaking. I will them to stop but that only makes them shake even more.

"Let's have a seat on the couch," he says as he grabs the bottle of wine by the neck.

I follow behind his cute butt into the expansive sitting room and sit down on the couch beside him. My hands are almost full-blown twitching as I hold the glass. Hopefully, the alcohol level of this wine is high enough to calm my nerves.

"So what would you like to know?" I ask.

He takes a sip of his wine and looks at me. "I want to get to know the assistant who will be working in my home. I don't really know much about you and you don't really know much about me except what you have read in magazines, half of which is false."

"I don't believe the stuff that's in magazines anyway," I say, only half telling the truth.

In reality, I really loved the gossip magazines, especially if my favorite celebrity was in there. It didn't matter if the story was true or not, I just really wanted to be entertained.

"Well that's good. You would be the first person I met who didn't," he says as he takes another sip of wine.

I take a big sip. More like a slurp.

Not classy at all.

I refocus on staying classy but I catch a waft of his cologne. The scent is intoxicating.

"If you want me to tell you something about me, you have to tell me a little bit about yourself first. There aren't any pictures of your family in here or friends. All I see is pictures of you from business and stuff like that."

He picks up his wine glass and drinks it all. "I'm not really close with my parents… or anyone in my family for that matter."

"Why not?" I press.

He looks off at the wall and then looks at me in my eyes.

"My mom and dad used to beat me."

His statement is blunt and full of pain. It catches me off-guard.

"I'm sorry to hear that," I reply.

I definitely hadn't read that in any of the gossip magazines.

"They used to beat me a lot. For no reason at all, other than the fact that they wanted to. One of my earliest memories is my father's hand coming down onto my face. I thought it was normal until I went to school and found out that my friends weren't beaten by their parents. But my parents continued to beat me until I was old enough to stand up for myself."

"That's horrible."

"I cut them off. They don't deserve to be any part of my success. I haven't seen them in many years."

He pours another glass of wine and takes a big gulp.

That explains why he is so withdrawn, I suppose. It would be hard to form a trusting relationship after experiencing that as a child.

All the gossip magazines label Brock as a mischievous rich playboy, but I have seen something that they haven't – vulnerability. He's not a playboy, he just doesn't know how to form a relationship.

The fact that he has opened up to me already makes me feel special.

"I can't imagine a parent doing that to their child or any child having to deal with that. That's awful," I say as Brock pours another glass of wine for me.

"A psychologist said that it is the reason I behave the way I do. They said that I like to be in control because I had no control in my childhood."

"Do you believe that?"

"Not at all. The psychologist was looking for a reason to explain behavior and that's what he chose. There's no proof that's the reason. I feel like it is all made up."

"But you do like to be in control?"

"I like to be in control because I love the power. I love the feeling of being powerful. That has nothing to do with my childhood."

"If you say so," I reply.

"But that doesn't matter anymore. I'm grown up now. I'm doing well for myself and they're still stuck in their tiny little apartment in the suburbs. That's the best revenge."

"You don't need to get revenge on them," I say without thinking.

Brock looks away from me and I can feel the tension in the air.

"Tell me something about you," he changes the conversation.

I take a sip of the delicious wine and try to think of something to tell him.

I have no deep dark secrets.

My parents love me and in fact, they still visit on a regular basis but there's no way I am going to tell him that.

"The library is my favorite place in the city. I like to spend hours there becoming one with the books and getting lost in another world. It's my place. It's where I feel at home."

He laughs. "So you're a little book worm? I never would've guessed. You don't really seem like the type to be sitting in a library curled up in a book."

"A lot of people say that but there is nothing more I love than being wrapped up in a book. It's all about escapism and entertainment."

He looks at me with a strange look in his eyes as he takes a sip of his wine.

It's almost as if he desires me but I could also be tipsy from my own glasses of wine. You are supposed to sip at expensive wine but here I am gulping it down by the mouthful.

"Bella. I need you to let me do something to you," Brock's tone drops lower.

His silky voice sends chills down my spine.

"What's that?" I ask nervously.

"I need you to be tied up. Naked."

Chapter 6

I gasp.

Of all the things I was expecting him to say, that was not one of them.

"You want to do what?"

Maybe, just maybe, I'd heard him wrong.

I had drunk two glasses of wine. Of course, I heard him wrong.

There is no way my new boss would say that to me.

"I said I need to tie you up naked to my bed," he states again.

His voice is so firm.

So direct.

I look at him and my pulse quickens.

I know that it's unprofessional to have sex with your boss even if it's what I have been thinking ever since I laid eyes on him but I didn't actually think that it would happen.

I take two more big gulps of wine and look at him in his eyes.

Without thinking, I reply.

"Okay."

He raises his brow. "Okay what?"

"Okay. You can tie me up in the bed."

A naughty smirk drifts across his handsome face.

This was not a good idea.

No way.

But how could I say no?

Brock motions for me to follow him into the bedroom. I realize at this point that I do not know how to say no to him. His dominance over me is clear.

His broad shoulders lead me through the apartment and into his bedroom.

Oh wow...

I thought that the apartment was impressive – but the bedroom is another level.

His bedroom is bigger than my apartment.

A sprawling bed covered in silk sheets lay in the middle of the room, with four tall bedposts surrounding it. It's white and black and looks as if he took the time to make sure that everything stayed in its place.

It's the stuff dreams are made of.

"Take off your clothes," he says in a voice that's deeper than his normal tone. "Now."

I submit to his demands.

Dropping down to my underwear, I stand before him. Exposed. My female curves are open for him to judge.

"All of it," he states, referring to the underwear remaining on my body.

I stare at him.

I don't know why but the nerves have gone. Maybe I'm too shocked to be feeling nervous?

Or maybe there is nothing here to be nervous about...

Slowly, I remove my underwear and bare my naked body to him.

Brock's eyes slowly drink in every curve.

I am a woman – the way we are supposed to be. I have breasts, curves and sensuality to match.

And by the bulge in Brock's trousers, I can tell that is what he likes.

"What do..." I start to say something but he puts his large hand over my mouth.

"Lay on the bed," he commands.

Completely naked in this vast penthouse bedroom, I walk and lay down on the bed.

Waiting.

Now the nerves return...

My heart is beating so hard that I can feel it in my mouth.

My limbs are weak with nerves.

Brock opens the drawer beside the bed and pulls out a set of ropes.

He looks at me and I don't say anything - I can't say anything - I just wait for him to do whatever it is that he wants to do to me.

He holds one of my wrists and uses the rope to tie it to one on the bedposts, then ties the other hand to his other bedpost. He looks at me with a smirk and I become slightly turned on.

This is a game.

This is his sexual adventure.

I try to move one of my hands but it is tied in tight.

Oh yes...

This is really starting to turn me on.

I feel like a woman.

I am his sex toy.

His plaything.

And I think I like that...

He spreads my legs apart and tightly ties each ankle to a bedpost. I can't even bring my thighs together. He pulls a blindfold from the drawer and places it over my eyes, tying it up behind my hair.

I didn't agree to the blindfold...

Wow, this blindfold is thick.

The blindfold doesn't let in any light and I can't even make out a shadow in front of me.

Then I feel his fingers...

The sensation of his fingers dancing down my naked body sends shivers through me. All my senses are heightened here.

I feel alive.

I hear rustling and I assume that he's stripping out of his clothes. Damn blindfold. I would love to see his hot, naked body. I feel the bed sink down a little and some movement between my legs.

He kisses my thigh.

Oh…

It's slow and soft.

With this blindfold on, all my senses are heightened.

The kiss sends signals running all through my body. His lips are all I can feel. All my energy is focused on the soft, sensual touch of his mouth.

He moves up my body and places kisses along my neck and collarbone, and nips my earlobe, which sends shivers down my spine. He places his hand around my neck firmly and begins to lick around one of nipples before he takes the whole thing inside of his mouth.

I don't know where he's going to kiss next and it is sending me wild.

My body starts to writhe in pleasure but I still can't move which only heightens the sensation.

He switches his attention to my other nipple and repeats the same action except this time he bites it a little before he pulls up. He removes his hand from around my neck and kisses me down my stomach slowly swirling his tongue round my navel.

Oh…

My senses are in overload.

He kisses below my belly button and my senses start to go up the wall yet again. He licks the inside of my thighs and as much as I want to move, I can't.

My wrists pull hard against the ropes, but they are too tight. My head throws forward and I want to rip this blindfold off… but I can't.

I'm his.

I am all his.

He kisses each of my thighs tenderly.

"Oh, you're so wet already," Brock moans.

I can feel his breath on my wet pussy.

And then…

Oh…

Two fingers slide deep inside me while his tongue licks around my navel.

Oh, I'm wet.

It feels so good to have his fingers inside me.

My senses are so alive!

He replaces his hand with his mouth and starts to slowly lick me. He traces every inch of my center before plunging his tongue deep inside of me.

Oh...

My whole body spasms with the intensity.

He starts to go slow at first and then he begins to tongue fuck me faster and faster.

His wet tongue sends feelings pulsating through every part of me.

Yes!

Fuck yes!

My body is in full overdrive and I don't how much more that I can take but I'm willing to find out. I have no choice.

I have never had an experience like this before.

My body squirms and I pull hard against the ropes but I am tied in tight.

I want to pull away... but I can't.

He owns me.

Yes!

I try to pull away. I don't know how high this will take me.

Then…

His tongue moves away.

Oh…

I need it back on me.

"Please," I whisper, "Come back."

I don't know where he is.

I can't see him and I can't feel him.

Where is he?

I feel a pressure at my opening and I gasp.

All the breath is drained from my body.

He enters me.

"Yes!" I scream as my head throws back.

I am completely filled with his cock.

Oh, he feels big.

He drives into my body slowly at first, giving me a chance to adjust to him but then he speeds up his strokes and sends my body into overdrive.

I scream out in pleasure as my head becomes dizzy with orgasm but he continues stroking me, going deeper and harder, sending me completely over the edge.

Deeper he pushes.

Oh, he feels so big inside me.

When he is inside me, I feel full. It feels like he is supposed to be there.

"Yes," I continue to moan as he plays with my breasts.

Then… he pumps harder.

Faster.

"Yes!"

He drives deeper into me.

My whole body shakes as the heat flushes over me in waves. Yes…

My head throws back again and my body shakes with orgasm.

"Yes!"

Brock stiffens… and then I can feel his warm seed entering me.

His deep, passionate moan echoes around the room.

I feel a weight shift on the bed, some rustling sounds, and then sound of a zipper being zipped up.

My head is still dizzy as Brock unties the ropes from my arms and legs and then removes the blindfold from around my face.

Wow...

That was incredible.

I look up at him and smile but he just stares blankly back at me.

"You can go home now," he says as he walks out of the room and shuts the door.

What?

I stare at the door in disbelief.

In a daze, I grab my clothes up off of the floor and get dressed.

Is he serious?

Walking into the living room, I look around for Brock but I don't see him. He was serious. In shock, I hit the button on the service elevator and press the button to go down to the parking garage.

What the hell just happened? ▯

Chapter 7

I pull into the driveway in shock, still confused about what happened, and I see all of the apartment lights are still on.

That is odd because it was almost twelve o'clock and usually around this time Naomi is sleeping, or if she waits up for me, it is usually just the kitchen light on.

When I quietly enter our place, I see Naomi sitting on the chair watching a scary movie with a big bowl of popcorn on her lap. She is so engrossed in the television that she doesn't hear me enter.

SLAM!

I slam the door and she jumps making the popcorn fly. I smile as she looks back at me and shoots me a death glare.

"Why did you do that?" she exclaims. "You do know that I could've killed you!"

"What were you going to kill me with? A bowl of popcorn?" I say with a laugh as I watch her pick popcorn out of her hair.

The laugh helps ease my confusion about the night.

"Where have you been? It's almost midnight," she asks as she sits the bowl down. "I thought that we could have a movie night together but you just waltz in here all late so I had to just watch them without you. Well one because I didn't make it to the other ones yet."

"I had to work late," I say as I place my keys and purse down on the table and walk into the kitchen.

"You don't work in the office anymore - you work in house so what could you possibly be working late on?" she asks with a raised brow.

"Brock wanted to get to know me a little better, that's all."

I can feel my cheeks turning red and I try to fight it.

"In what way did he want to get to know you?"

I go quiet, which only makes Naomi's eyes get wide and she rushes into the kitchen after me.

"Did you guys? You know. Did you two do the dirty deed? Dancing in the sheets? The nasty nasty."

"Yes," I say bluntly.

"What?!" her eyes almost pop out of her head. "With your boss?"

I needed to talk about it with someone and who better to talk about it with than my best friend.

Naomi pulls out a chair and rests her chin on her hand.

"Well give me all of the details. I want to know *everything*."

"We started off drinking wine and he was telling me about his childhood and I told him that I love the library and books," I sigh.

"You admitted to him that you were a book nerd? What were you thinking? You don't tell guys that," she says as she rolls her eyes.

"Yes I did tell him and he found it to be attractive, thank you very much. Now, do you want the story or not?" I ask her.

"Okay. Okay. Carry on. You were having a boring conversation and then what?"

"He was all rich and charming and then he was like, 'I want to tie you up naked to my bed.'"

"What?!"

I nod.

"He just came out and asked you, can I tie you up to my bed?" she exclaims.

I roll my eyes at her.

"Sorry," she says as she fans herself with her hand, "Okay geez, carry on but the story is getting juicy already. The guy has balls."

"Okay so he was like, I want to tie you up naked to my bed, and I thought if I don't do this then I might lose my job. So I agreed. He tied me up to his bed and put a blindfold on."

"And then?" her eagerness for the rest of the story is clear.

"And it was *so* amazing. I loved the way that he dominated me. I have never experienced that before. He was a real man and I was treated like a real woman... I don't know if it's a feeling I can explain," I say, waiting for her to freak out even more.

"So you're a little closet freak?" she asks with a laugh. "I always knew beneath that little bookworm act that you were a freak. I just didn't know it would take your boss to bring that out of you."

"What! I have never done anything like that a day in my life. I did it to keep my job."

"That's the only reason you did it?"

"Yes… no… I don't know."

"You enjoyed it?" she presses.

"I really enjoyed it and I do mean, *really* enjoyed it. He was like the perfect fit to my body. Almost as if he were made just for me," I say my voice trailing off a little as I think about my experience with him all over again.

I don't want to tell her that he left right after our moment.

I am embarrassed about it. Right now, the night sounds amazing to Naomi and I want to keep it that way.

Maybe Brock just had something to do?

He is a really busy man. Maybe he just ran out of time?

And if I admit that he left, then it becomes real.

"So did he say that if you didn't let him tie you up that you would be fired?" she asks.

"No, he didn't say that I would be fired but that doesn't mean that I wouldn't have been. But he'd probably think that I'd sue him for sexual harassment or something."

"So therefore you did it because you wanted to. All those romance novels finally got to you, huh? Wanted to steam up your life a little bit? I don't blame you though. It's been quite a while since you've seen some action."

I laugh. "The man is hot. There is no denying that. I was given an opportunity and I took it. If you were in my position you would've done the same thing."

"You're right about that but that's right up my alley. I like things like that. You, on the other hand, have always been so vanilla," she says.

"I guess now I can be considered rocky road."

"More like marshmallow fluff."

We look at each other and burst into laughter.

"I really did enjoy it though. I didn't know that sex could be so good when you don't participate and have the other person in control."

Naomi nods her head. "It's called being a submissive or a sub. It's when you allow someone to dominant you in the bedroom."

"They have words for things like these?"

"What have you been doing? Living in the dark ages?"

I laugh. "No, but I've just been having regular sex. If you want to call it regular sex."

"So in other words it's boring sex."

I laugh. "It's just sex."

"So are you going to be tied up by him again?"

I shrug my shoulders. "For all I know, it could have been a one-time thing."

She looks at me in my eyes and smirks. "But if he asks again will you do it?"

I look at her, at the floor and then back at her. "If he wants to… I wouldn't object."

She claps her hands, laughing. "And the baby freak is born!"

I roll my eyes again. "I'm going to bed. I have to get up in the morning."

"I bet. All the better to get back to Brock McHottie."

I laugh and head towards my bedroom.

Flipping on the light switch, I take a long look at myself in the mirror. I see that I now have a certain glow about me that I didn't have before and I like it.

I slide out of my clothes and pull on my pajamas, hit the light switch, and hop into bed. I toss and turn because I can't fall asleep. I keep thinking of Brock tying me up to his bed and controlling me.

It was so sexy.

So damn sexy.

It was blissful and I enjoyed every minute of it.

My body starts to get hot just thinking about it. Hot damn. Nobody has ever made me feel this way before.

Then my mind starts to go through the reasons why he might have left straight afterwards. He must have a reason.

There must be some reason why he left...

I look over at the clock and it reads two-thirty in the morning. I have to be to work tomorrow at nine and I know that I would never get up if I didn't get any sleep right now. I toss and turn for a while longer but I finally get to sleep with thoughts of Brock still floating around in my mind.

My alarm shocks me out of my sleep and I roll over to shut it off.

I look at my phone and see that I have a text from Brock saying that I can have the weekend off because he has an unexpected business trip and that he will see me Monday.

With a sigh I fall back into my pillow.

I hope that's true.

I hope that he's not avoiding me...

Chapter 8

Naomi comes into the living room and sees me sitting on the chair drinking my morning coffee.

"I thought that you had to work today," she says as she sits beside me.

"Off for the weekend. Apparently, Brock had a last minute business trip," I say as I take another sip of my coffee.

"Why do you sound so down? Wanted to get some more action in, huh?" she says with a nudge.

"Um…" I shrug my shoulders, "I was just really looking forward to seeing him. Plus, I really like the job."

"You don't have to lie to me. I know that you were looking forward to getting tied up again."

I laugh. "I wasn't. Like I said, I just really enjoy the job."

She smirks. "And all of the benefits that come along with it."

"Not complaining."

"Hell, I wouldn't either if my job had benefits like yours but all my boss cares about is driving us all crazy so that she doesn't have to actually do any work herself. She's such a witch!"

"But you love your job."

"Yeah I do. I'm not too fond of working for a monster though."

I laugh again. "So are you cooking breakfast?"

"I would but with the week I've had, I'm going to eat out," she says. "You want to join me?"

"That depends. Where are we getting breakfast from? I don't really like to eat at those weird hippy places you love."

"I like to try everything at least once, vanilla... And apparently so do you."

I roll my eyes. "So where are we going?"

"Pancake house?"

I smile. "My favorite place in the world."

She giggles and gets up from the chair. "You do know that you sounded like a little kid when you said that right?"

I laugh. "The pancake house has the tendency to do that to me."

She shakes her head and grabs her purse. After a short trip to our breakfast spot, we are greeted by the smell of fluffy pancakes and bacon.

This was the best pancake shop in the city but not many people knew about it because it was tucked away from the main street.

We take a seat at a booth in the back and a waitress brings over a menu but neither of us take a look because we know what we're going to get.

"I'll have a strawberry pecan pancake short stack with a side of bacon and scrambled eggs," I order.

"And I'll have the chocolate chip pancake short stack with sausage and hash browns," says Naomi.

"And we'll both take orange juice."

The waitress smiles at us and leaves the table with our order.

"Maybe we come in here too much?" says Naomi.

I shake my head. "No, we don't come in here enough."

This is our comfort spot.

Whenever one of us was going through something, we would come here and pig out on pancakes. Or whenever we wanted to celebrate… or just because.

Truth was we were both pancake fanatics and this was the best place in town to get them. The waitress comes back and places our orange juice on the table and I take a sip from it.

"So what do you have planned today?" I ask Naomi.

She takes a sip. "Nothing was going to sit in the house all day and finish watching the movies I rented."

"Want some company?"

"Sure who better to have a movie day with than my best friend?"

The waitress places our orders on the table and I grab the warm syrup from her hand and pour it over everything on my plate. Naomi grabs the syrup and just pours it over her pancakes. As I take a bite of my pancakes, my eyes roll in the back of my head.

These pancakes get better every time I taste them.

They are heaven. Pure bliss on a plate.

My plate is empty in no time.

"He didn't talk to me after it," I blurt out, not able to keep it a secret any longer.

"Really?" Naomi enquires. "Not a word?"

"He told me to get dressed and leave."

She nods knowingly.

"What?" I question.

"That is known to happen. Sometimes, when exploring a deep, dark fantasy, men feel dirty after it is finished. I think it's in their genetic make-up. Don't take it personally."

"How can I not take it personally? That was the most personal experience of my life."

"If you play with the fire, you have to be prepared to get burnt."

"My pain threshold isn't as high as yours. I hurt easily, Naomi."

She frowns, "Sounds like you need a day on the couch. Come on, let's go and choose some movies."

Maybe it is normal for a man to leave straight after an intense experience?

If it is, I'm not sure I can do it again.

I don't like feeling alone after a passionate session of lovemaking.

I like the man to stay with me and hold my body tightly in his warm arms.

I like to know that I am loved.

"I know the perfect movie for you," Naomi smiles. "It will keep your mind off your adventure before Monday."

And that is the reason Naomi is my best friend.

She knows me better than anyone.

⁂

Chapter 9

After a weekend in front of the television, I wake up at six o'clock Monday morning eager to get to work.

After taking a quick shower, I throw on some clothes, grab my keys and rush out of the house. In the parking garage of Brock's penthouse, I check my reflection one last time in the rearview mirror.

I can do this.

I have to do this.

If I want to keep this job, I have to go back in there.

Butterflies flutter in my stomach and I start to ring my hands as I stand at the elevator door.

Damn.

I don't know what to do.

What if he doesn't want me?

What if last time was a one-time thing? What if he didn't enjoy it?

Am I going upstairs to get fired?

Or does he really expect everything to go back to normal after the night that we had?

The door to the elevator opens and Brock is standing in the kitchen with a smirk on his face.

"Good morning, sir," I nervously say as I step off of the elevator.

He doesn't say anything.

His eyes dance down my body and then back up.

And then he nudges his head towards the bedroom.

Without a response from me, he walks that way.

Tentatively, I follow him into the room where he closes the door behind us.

"Take off your clothes," he demands.

What?

I'm not ready for this.

"Um... this early in the morning?" I question in surprise.

"Yes."

His response is so firm.

How do I say no to that?

Nerves flush all over my body.

"Um..." I try to think of something to say.

But I can't.

I can't think of anything to say.

"Take them off."

He instructs me with his firm voice.

My heart rate is pounding so fast that I am frozen stiff.

"Now."

The firmness in his voice increases.

Like the good little girl that I am, I do as I'm told.

I drop my jacket on the floor, pull down my tight skirt and unbutton my shirt.

"Good," Brock's silky voice moans as he walks behind me.

His hands unclip my bra from behind while his breath whispers on my shoulder.

I can't move.

I'm too nervous.

His strong hands run over my hips and push my underwear to the floor.

I'm naked.

Again.

I nervously wait for him to say something else…

My body is already a rush of emotion and I can feel my senses tingling.

"Lay down on the bed," he demands.

I lay my naked body on the bed and he begins to tie me up again…

Only this time he leaves the blindfold in the drawer.

As he tightens the ropes around my wrists, he leans down beside me and licks my ear lobe, shooting tingles through my skin.

Oh…

He leans over and licks the other one and nips it with his teeth.

"I want to play a game with you."

I nod my head.

"I'm going to leave you in this room all day… tied up to my bed like this. I will have the door locked so no one can enter. I will come in and out of here all day giving you pleasure and when I am done I will release you. Do you understand?"

I nod my head like a nice girl.

"Good."

He places a kiss on my lips and licks me slowly up and down my neck and I moan in pleasure. Then he gets up from the bed and walks out of the room.

I see the lock turn.

I am completely naked and vulnerable.

I am his.

I have never been in this type of position before.

But I like it...

When I took the job I thought that I would be doing mundane things but if I knew this would happen I would've asked to work at his penthouse sooner...

I love the thrill of being tied to his bed and having him dominant me and I wonder if it could lead to anything more or was it just a sex thing?

An hour slowly ticks past.

I'm getting restless.

Come back already.

The lock to the door turns…

I really hope that it's Brock coming in.

His large, strong frame comes through the door.

Brock walks in with a cup in his hand and a smirk on his face. He gently places the cup on the table, never quite taking his eyes off me.

Out of the cup, he pulls out an ice-cube.

Gently, he runs the ice-cube across my lips…

Oh…

The chill dances through my whole body.

Yes…

Brock looks down at me and smirks.

I want him.

He takes the ice-cube and slowly rubs it up and down my neck until it melts. The chill drips onto my skin, melting the lust into me.

Oh…

He gets two more ice cubes and circles my nipples with them.

My nipples immediately get hard and the pleasure that is running through my body is almost unbearable.

He grabs the cup of ice and goes to the edge of the bed.

Brock leans down between my legs and places a piece of ice between his lips. Lying on the bed, he rubs the ice up and down my clit and I moan in pleasure.

Yes…

I can't help it. He owns me.

He then slips a piece of ice deep inside of my opening and follows it up with his tongue.

My mind is blank.

My body is alive.

"Yes…" I moan deeply.

He starts to lick me and my legs start to shake from the pleasure.

Just as I'm starting to lose control, he removes his tongue.

Without another word, he stops, picks up the cup and walks back out of the room.

Was that it?

Oh man… this is going to be a long day.

I sigh and wonder what else he has planned for the day but also wonder how long he plans to have me tied up here.

I know that he said all day but he couldn't possibly mean it... could he?

After all, I'm pretty sure that my arms and legs would eventually get tired from being tied to the bed all day.

Two hours slowly tick past...

My mouth is starting to get dry and my stomach starts to grumble from hunger.

I stare at the latch on the door, willing for it to open.

But it doesn't.

Time ticks by and he still doesn't come into the room.

After another hour passes, the latch on the door finally turns.

Brock walks into the room with a tray and a cup of water. He sits on the edge of the bed, loosens the ties on my hands enough to allow me to sit up, and passes a sandwich to me.

He puts a glass of water to my mouth and I sip from it.

He doesn't say anything and I don't say anything either.

What is there to say?

I just continue to let him feed me and give me something to drink.

Once I'm done with the sandwich, he starts to undress his magnificent body. I didn't get to see it on Friday night because my eyes were blindfolded but looking at him now - he is stunning.

The more clothes that come off him, the wetter I become.

He has rock hard abs and a cock that could rival a horse.

He is perfect in every way and I want to drink in his presence so that I don't forget a single thing.

He kneels his body over my face and places his cock by my lips.

"Open your mouth."

I do as I'm told and he sticks his cock deep inside my mouth, and starts to pump in and out of me.

His strong hands hold my hair as he thrusts into me.

Oh...

His hard cock is so big.

He pumps faster.

Harder.

And then...

Yes...

He comes deep inside my throat and I swallow his seed.

Oh...

He withdraws his large cock from my mouth and I moan as he does.

And all I can think is I hope that he gives it to me one more time like that because I think that I'm becoming addicted to him...

Chapter 10

I watch him as he begins to dress that amazing body.

After he has loosely put on his shirt, he removes the ropes from around my arms and legs, letting me free.

A smile is stretched across my face as I stare at him.

"That was amazing," I say as I sit up on the bed.

He looks at me but doesn't say anything.

"Do you want to talk?" I question in hope.

He stares at me for a while and walks out of the room.

I stare after him in disbelief.

My dizzying high comes to a crashing low. Damn. He has left me again.

I feel cold without his presence next to me.

How could he still not want me after all that's going on with us?

What am I to him?

Just some useless girl?

A throw away?

Some random piece of booty just to use whenever he feels like it?

I can feel the tears welling up in my eyes but I refuse to let them fall.

Bastard.

I can't do this.

I can't ride this rollercoaster of passion.

As wild as it is, I want to get off this ride.

In my moment of despair, I make a decision.

Today is going to be my last day here at this job because there is no way that I can just sit here and let him treat me this way.

I put my clothes back on and look around the room for a piece of paper and a pen to write with. I find what I'm looking for on his dresser.

And begin my letter…

Brock,

I can't do this anymore. You are giving me mixed signals and I just can't deal with that or be around you. You're so cold and I don't know what you're doing to me but I don't like it one bit.

Today is my last day.

Goodbye,

Bella.

I rip off the piece of paper and place it on his bed so that he will see it before he goes to sleep. I want to tell him to his face that I quit, but I know I'll never have enough nerve to do that.

I grab my purse and keys off of his dresser and head to the service elevator. I look around the room for Brock but I don't see him.

I press the button to the garage and as soon as the door closes, I feel tears falling down my face.

I wipe them away but they just keep falling.

My exit from the garage is fast. I want to get as far away from this building and Brock as I possibly can.

I pull into my yard in record time and I'm glad to see Naomi's car in the driveway.

Chapter 11

"I quit my job!" I burst out as soon as I step into my apartment.

Naomi's face is covered in disbelief and she pushes her nail polish off to the side of the couch, leaving enough room for me to sit.

"You did what? Why? I mean…okay… but why? What happened? I thought that you really liked the job. Especially since you were getting extra benefits."

A deep sigh escapes my lungs as I sit down on the couch and think about what I'm going to say to her because it was all so crazy.

"Can I have a good cry first?" I ask her.

"Of course," Naomi pulls me into a warm hug and I pour tears onto her shoulder.

The tears flow heavily as my whole body lets out cries of rejection.

After having her shoulder soaked, Naomi pulls out of the hug, hands me a box of tissues and patiently waits for me to begin.

"As soon as I got to work this morning, Brock motioned for me to go into the bedroom with him so I went. I didn't think that he would want to have sex that early in the morning but if he did, then I wasn't going to stop him. He tied me up to the bed all day and was coming in and out of the room when he felt like it, stimulating me in different ways… And it was amazing… Mind blowing actually. He came in and kissed all of my body parts with so much passion, rubbed me down with ice, licked me, sexed me senseless but then when I tried to talk to him afterwards… he just brushed me off like I was just another piece of flesh."

"Oh, sweetie…"

"I can't deal with that, Naomi. I can't. I'm not the type of person who can just keep having sex with no personal interaction."

"So what did you do?"

"I left him a note saying that I quit. He'll see it before he goes to sleep. I didn't have enough nerve to quit face to face."

She stares at me with her mouth open and then she shuts it. Her eyes stare blankly at me as she thinks about what she wants to say to me next.

"He had you tied up to the bed from the moment you walked in the house up until a little while ago?" she asks.

I nod my head.

I don't have the nerve to say anything else. It was all too crazy.

Naomi was trying hard to digest the story that I was telling her.

"And then when it's all said and done, you didn't even get a thank you? No 'I'll see you tomorrow'?"

I shake my head. "I don't think he listened to a single word I said."

"That dude is a jerk if I ever heard one!" Naomi reacts to my pain. "Look maybe he didn't really need a personal assistant for his house, he just wanted to get laid and by you saying that you would do anything to keep your job, he just took advantage of the situation. What a jerk!"

"It's my fault," I whisper.

"No. It's not!" Naomi snaps back, "He's an asshole and you deserve so much better. I know my boss isn't perfect but if she ever pulled anything like this, we would have had her fired on the spot. I still can't believe you didn't wait around to tell him to his face. That's what I would've done and he would've deserved it. Plain and simple."

I sigh and draw patterns on the couch with my finger.

"I hate to say this… but… the problem is while I was lying there spread eagle on his bed, I was thinking that I could get used to this. That I could get used to him dominating me in the bedroom and being tied up to things. He had me thinking that because we were doing this all day that it would change something between us... and in a way it did. It has opened my eyes to not have sex with my boss ever again and to not put that much trust into a man again. It's asking for trouble. I'll stick to the romance books and living adventurously through the people in the stories I read."

"You were developing feelings for him, weren't you?" she asks as she takes my hand into hers.

I shrug my shoulders, "I think so. But how do you know? I felt a connection with him and he opened up to me about his past. I thought that we had something... I could tell that he didn't share that with anyone or that he has never opened up to anyone in his life before he talked to me on the chair. But ever since that one night, he has barely said anything to me other than command me around in the bedroom. I wanted more nights like that one but I know now that it'll never happen. I'm starting to think that it was all part of his plan."

"He's a rich jerk."

"I'm not even sure that he listened to a word I said. I was a plaything for him. Nothing more," I try to convince myself that it was true.

"I think that you're better off without him and besides, you've got me. I'm always here for you. I know that I can't dominate you in the bedroom but I can be your shoulder to lean on when you need it and make you laugh and smile when need be."

"Thanks," I smile through my teary face.

"I know that this can't be easy and I want you to know that you have my full support. I'm even ready if you want to go back to his penthouse and slap him and give him a piece of your mind. That is what I really think you should do but since you're the reserved one, I know that it's not going to happen. Today."

"I'm surprised you didn't say anything about us going to be homeless and have to dumpster dive out of trashcans and stuff," I say trying to steer the subject elsewhere. "I know that you've been worried a lot about that lady at work and I don't want to send you into full panic mode now that I'm not working anymore right now. All I could think was to get the hell out of there, not how it would affect us both in the long run. If you want me to move out, I understand."

She looks at me and laughs. "I have enough saved up to cover you until you get another job but don't wait too long to get one or we will be fighting a homeless guy over a half-eaten chicken. And as I said before, I don't think we'll make it out there on the streets. We are too pretty and neither one of us is really street smart. Probably have to find a crazy lady who pushes a buggy to show us the ropes."

I look at her and roll my eyes. "That's never going to happen right? You're scared of that old lady who pushes the grocery buggy because you say that she talks to cats and spits on people."

"I'm playing but are you sure that you're okay? I can understand if you got hurt. With a guy like that I'm sure any girl would fall for him a little. I probably would have done too if I were you. Sometimes you just fall for someone without having any control over your emotions. I know how that feels. Especially with everything that happened with Trey. I fell for him and he broke my heart into a million little pieces. It took me a while to heal but I did. I healed and you will to."

I nod my head.

"I'm good, but I need to take a hot bath and climb into bed."

"If you need anything just please let me know. I'm here for you, Bella," she says.

I smile at her and squeeze her hand. "Thank you."

The bathroom is my beautiful sanctuary. It's the place where I can escape the pain outside these walls. I pour ample amounts of my favorite honey and milk bubble bath into the tub and indulge in the luxurious smell.

As I strip down, I catch a glimpse of my refection in the mirror.

The glow that was once there is gone and now I see a woman who looks like a sad puppy. My wrists are still marked with the rope burns from when I was trying to fight the pleasure that was running through my body.

I slip into the bath and the soaking hot water begins to relax my tired body.

In the moments of relaxation, my mind starts to wander to Brock, his amazing physique and the way he feels inside me.

Damn.

I shake my head and try to lose the thoughts.

"Snap out of it, girl. He's no good for you," I say to myself.

I lay back deeper into the tub and soon all thoughts of Brock are gone and all I can think of is peace. The soft water feels amazing and my body is content.

I hide in the solitude of the tub until my fingers start to prune and the water turns cold.

When I land in bed, the thoughts of his body come back. Even in here, in my bed, I can't escape the thoughts of Brock that are racing through my mind. Grabbing my music player, I put in the ear buds and put on my loudest playlist to distract me but after twenty minutes, I realize that it won't work either.

Turning off my lamp, I place my head in my pillow and cry until I have no tears left.

First thing tomorrow morning I am definitely going to the library because I need to escape my mind and that's the only way that I know how to do it...

[?]

Chapter 12

The morning sun streams through my curtains, waking me from my slumber.

Rolling over to look at the clock, it takes a few moments for my eyes to adjust to the bright digital display. When my eyes finally adapt to the light, I realize that it reads eleven o'clock in the morning.

I have slept most of my morning away and I don't feel bad about it all.

Not after the night I had.

My arm reaches as far as it can stretch, grabbing my cellphone off the small bedside table. Reading the display, I see three missed calls from Brock.

Really?

Couldn't he find another booty call to satisfy his needs?

The calls make the anger burn inside me. How dare he call me?

I want nothing more to do with that man. Heartless bastard.

Shaking my head, I block his number from calling my phone again. There is no way that I am going to let it happen again.

That man took my heart, played with it, and then squashed it with his overpriced and fancy shoes.

What a bastard.

I am not a plaything and I never will be.

I am more than that.

Rolling out of bed, I don't even bother to glance at myself in the mirror because I know I look a mess. I make my way into the kitchen and see a doughnut with sprinkles on it, along with a note from Naomi.

Thought that you would need something sweet to start your day with. See you when I get home.

Naomi.

I smile and take a bite of the doughnut.

It is just what I need.

The right taste of sweet and greasy.

After avoiding it for as long as I can, I finally look at myself in the mirror. My eyes look tired and my skin looks worn but other than that, presentable to the world.

Making my way out to my car, I start the engine with an aggressive roar and begin my drive to the library.

Ah, the library.

My safe haven.

Walking into the beautiful building, the smell of well-read books greets me. It's hard to explain what I feel when I'm in the library but it's pure bliss.

I am surrounded by stories of love, heartbreak, and adventure.

Knowing that the world is full of stories makes me feel my story isn't as overwhelming.

Walking over to the romance section, I grab a couple of books that interest me off the shelf and I get my usual table in the far back corner where no one can disturb me.

It's just me and the books.

The first novel is from one of my favorite authors, so I know that it's good.

And if anything, it's sure to keep my mind off the jerk, who played with my emotions so cheaply.

As I read the classic love story, I can't help but imagine Brock as the main character.

Damn.

This man seems to be everywhere.

Why can't I just forget him?

Why can't I choose who I fall for?

I get a few chapters in when I feel someone's eyes on me.

Can't I get even a few moments of silence!

Grrr…

And then I look up…

Chapter 13

Brock Maxton.

Tall. Broad. Seductive.

Dominant.

And standing in front of me.

"What are you doing here?" I ask him angrily as I place the book down on the table.

"I came here to talk to you," he says as he takes a seat in front of me.

"How did you know that I was here?"

"Your favorite place in the world is the library."

"Where did you find that out?" I snap back, "Did you break into my social media accounts to find out my personal information?"

"No. You told me."

"You actually listened to me?" I question in surprise.

"Yes," a smirk comes across his face.

"So why do you want to talk now?" I shake my head. "When I wanted to talk to you, you seemed otherwise occupied."

"I told you from the start that it was hard for me to form relationships with people. I'm a closed individual but..."

He doesn't finish the sentence.

"But?" I question him.

"But you're different. I felt a pull to you."

"A pull? That's the best you've got? You're going to have to do better than that if you want to talk to me again."

"I didn't fire you when you first spilled coffee all over my files on your first day because I knew you were special."

"Special is getting better."

"Really special."

I shake my head at him.

"Really exceptional," he states.

"You're not good at this, are you?" I can't help it but a smirk comes over my face.

"No," his eyes drop to the table.

"What exactly do you want from me, Brock?"

He stares at me. He doesn't know the answer.

"Because I'm not down to just be your booty call," my finger hits the table, "You set something off inside of me Brock. You awakened a spirit that I didn't even know was there… and then you just stomped on it when you shut me out."

"I'm sorry," he takes a long pause. "You're perfect Bella. You're exactly what I've always wanted. You're a strong, vibrant woman but submissive in the bedroom. That's perfect."

I look at him and take in what he says.

Damn him and his seductive look…

I want to give him a chance but how can I trust what he says when he has so many issues?

How could I trust such a damaged soul?

"Look Brock, I want to give you a chance but I don't know. I don't think I can take that risk."

"I know that I'm difficult at times, but I'm telling you that it will be worth it."

Our eyes connect and I see deep within his soul.

My heart melts…

"Take the risk, Bella."

I pull my eyes away from his seductive stare and I try to think about what I should do.

But I can't.

I can't think about anything.

My mind is blank.

"Brock... if I take this chance you can't shut me out. We have to communicate."

He nods his head.

"And I'm not just going to be a booty call either."

"I'll take you out for a night on the town every week."

I raise my eyebrow. "I'm serious, Brock. I'm not in this just to be your plaything. I am not a toy."

He leans forward. "I'm not looking for you to be my play thing."

"Then we have a deal," I say with a smile.

"Good... because I have plans for us right now."

"And where will these plans take us?"

"To the bedroom."

My insides jump.

Oh yes...

?

Chapter 14

Brock's warm hand leads me out of the library and I can feel the butterflies in my stomach going bananas.

No man has ever made me feel the way that he has and I want that feeling to last forever.

I feel wanted.

I feel like a woman.

It seems like he is the one I've been waiting on my whole life. He is the hero from out of all the romance novels I've read.

But this was real life and real life as way more interesting than anything I've read in a book.

Especially now.

The world around me becomes a soft blur and before I know it, we're standing in Brock's spacious penthouse apartment, sipping beautiful wine again.

He talks to me casually, and I respond, but my mind is lost in all the nerves.

"Tonight... you get to touch me," he whispers in my ear after our third glass of wine.

"Really?" I ask as the nerves flood through me again.

Brock walks around behind me and his breath awakens parts of my body that until a week ago, I didn't know existed.

His hands run smoothly over my clothes and my heart rate increases with each passing moment.

He takes the shirt off my upper body, tossing it aside. His kisses land on my collarbone and I almost melt right there and then.

I lean backwards into his strength and as I press into him, I feel the bulge in his trousers. On instinct, I swing around and my hand gropes his groin. The swelling fills my grip.

"He wants to get free," I say to him before Brock engulfs me in a kiss filled with passion.

His hands hold my face while his kiss sends emotion surging through me.

Oh...

I pull away from his delicious mouth and drop to my knees. I race to pull open his belt, allowing his hard cock to be free.

His trousers and jocks drop in one motion and then I see it in all its glory.

Wow…

He's big.

The biggest I've ever seen.

I look at it in awe while both my hands wrap around his dick. I don't have big hands, but both my hands fit easily on the shaft and don't even come close to wrapping around it.

My tongue licks him and he tastes like man.

I take him deep in my mouth while my hands grip onto his hardness. My tongue runs along the shaft, covering him in salvia.

Wow…

I pump my hands up and down his shaft while my tongue licks his tip. Brock runs his strong hands through my hair and the faster my hands pump, the deeper he moans.

Oh yes…

My eyes look up to him and catch him watching me lavish his cock with praise. The smile on his face says it all.

He pulls his cock away from me and grabs me under the shoulders, moving my body onto the couch. He aggressively removes my remaining clothes and tosses them aside with distain.

He wants me.

He wants me bad.

I lay back on the soft leather couch and he kisses my lips passionately. His fingers find my wetness and he starts to touch me...

His strong touch sends electricity pulsating through my skin.

Oh...

Brock kisses my neck while he slips two fingers deep inside my opening.

I gasp when his fingers enter...

Yes...

My entire body clenches.

His fingers enter slowly, forcing my pussy to become even wetter.

He bends his head and takes one of my breasts into his mouth while slowly kneading the other one and then he switches. I moan in pleasure as I take in what he's doing. My whole body is on fire and I want nothing more than to yell - screw me already!

He pulls back and stares deep into my eyes.

I see him.

The real Brock Maxton.

Then...

He enters me.

Oh...

Yes...

His member penetrates deep into my wetness.

He slides in with tenderness...

Then out...

Slowly, he continues. Brock's eyes remain locked onto mine as he moves deep inside me.

Fuck...

Yes...

I can feel it build. My body is on fire.

Every inch of my skin burns with passion.

Then...

Yes...

It hits me.

Wave after wave. Flood after flood.

Sensational.

My mind is lost.

Every part of my mind is lost to Brock's passion.

He drives deep into me and I can feel him in places that I've never felt anyone before. He is filling me with his manhood and I love it.

This was meant to be…

"Bend over," Brock says as he withdraws from me.

I obey because I'll do anything to have him back inside me.

I bend over the couch and immediately he slams into my opening.

"Fuck!" I yell in surprise.

I have never been one to be noisy during sex, but this, I can't help. He owns me. I let out another low yell as he pounds deeper and faster into me.

Deeper!

Harder!

Oh!

I throw it back into him and I feel his body tense up.

His hands grip tighter. His fingers rip into me. His whole body flexes!

And then he surges one last time...

Oh...

His large frame slumps on the couch next to me.

This time, I snuggle into his warm body and his large arm wraps around, holding me safely.

"You don't have to go home tonight," he whispers. "I want you to stay with me."

Brock holds me in his arms for a long time – his warm body seducing me all over again.

I look up at him and my heart warms as I kiss him gently on the lips.

Yes...

This is where I belong...

?

Epilogue

One year later...

Brock and I walk into the library where we are welcomed as the guests of honor.

Some moments of the past year have been rough but we've made it through. Brock is always willing to learn and that's what I love about him.

Yes – Love.

I can say that now. I love him and he loves me.

There have been times where I've doubted whether it was enough but it has been.

We did it.

We have made it through the hard times.

We are at the library because we have donated one million dollars to redevelop the east wing, where we started dating. I talked Brock into it and he will pretty much do anything to keep me happy.

"Thank you both so much," the head librarian interrupts my thoughts. "Your donation will go a long way to attracting other people to the library because we needed the face life. The money will make an amazing difference to this place."

"It was our pleasure. Besides, with all the time my lovely girlfriend spends in here, it was an easy decision," says Brock.

I laugh. "I can't help it if I like to get cozy with a good book every now and then."

The librarian smiles. "You're welcome here anytime, Bella. We enjoy seeing you walk through the door."

"And I very much enjoy walking through the door."

She smiles and hugs us one more time before walking away and talking to the rest of the guests. We walk over towards the refreshment table and I grab a small finger sandwich before taking in the scenes.

A naughty thought sends a smile across my face.

"What are you thinking about?" Brock asks curiously.

"I'm thinking about you."

"Doing what?" he asks.

"Tying me up in the new library wing. There are rails on the new staircase..."

A large smile drifts across Brock's face, "I think there is a way that we can make that happen."

I wink at him.

"Yes please…"

The End

Authors Note:

Thank you for reading this story. I value your input, your thoughts and your opinions. If you loved this story, please leave a review and tell me!

A review means the world to an author – we work so hard on the stories we share with you.

If you enjoyed this story, please check out my fan favorite '*The Billionaire's Lust*.'

For my fans, I have already started on my next story...

Thank you!

Kelli Sloan

Also by Kelli Sloan:

Romance: Housekeeper for the Billionaire

Romance: The Billionaire's Lust

Romance: The Billionaire's Secrets

Romance: The Billionaire's Desire

Romance: Working for the Billionaire's Pleasure

Manufactured by Amazon.ca
Bolton, ON

14022394R00079